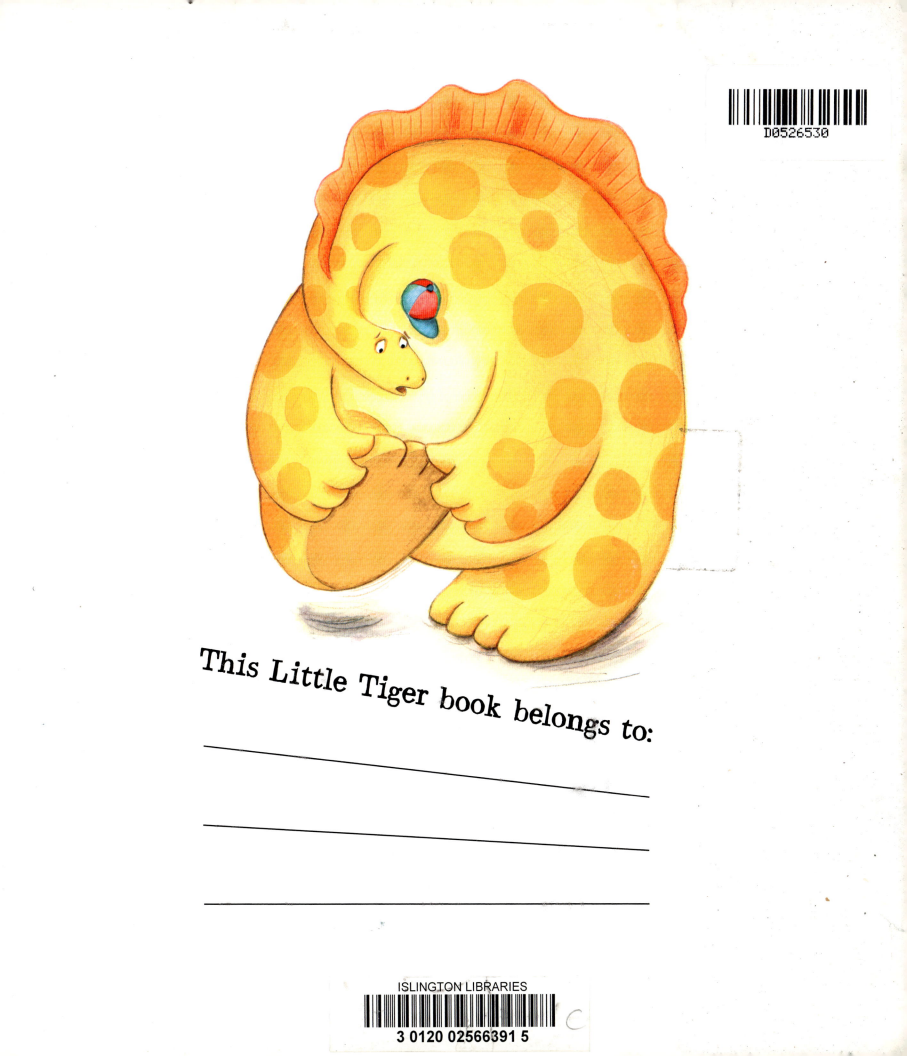

This Little Tiger book belongs to:

_____

_____

_____

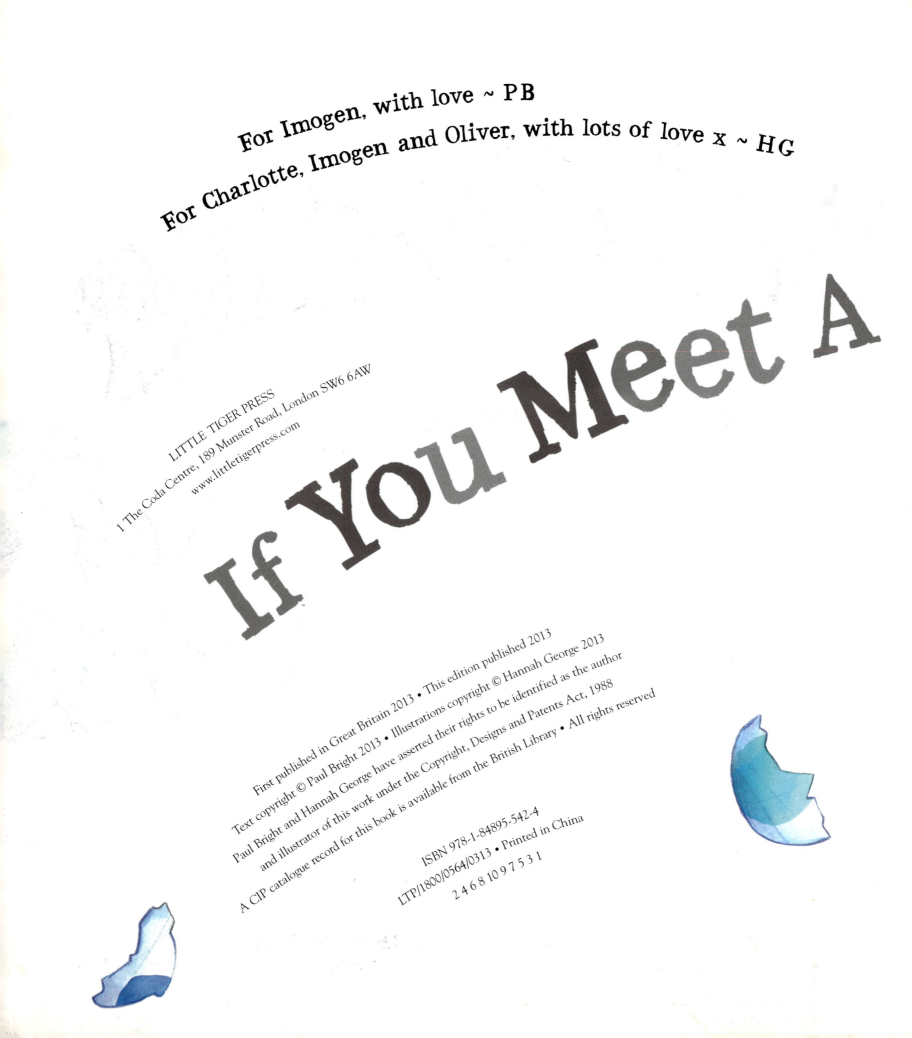

For Imogen, with love ~ P B

For Charlotte, Imogen and Oliver, with lots of love x ~ HG

If You Meet A

LITTLE TIGER PRESS

1 The Coda Centre, 189 Munster Road, London SW6 6AW

www.littletigerpress.com

First published in Great Britain 2013 • This edition published 2013

Text copyright © Paul Bright 2013 • Illustrations copyright © Hannah George 2013

Paul Bright and Hannah George have asserted their rights to be identified as the author

and illustrator of this work under the Copyright, Designs and Patents Act, 1988

A CIP catalogue record for this book is available from the British Library • All rights reserved

ISBN 978-1-84895-542-4 • Printed in China

LTP/1800/0564/0313

2 4 6 8 10 9 7 5 3 1

DINOSAUR

Paul Bright   Hannah George

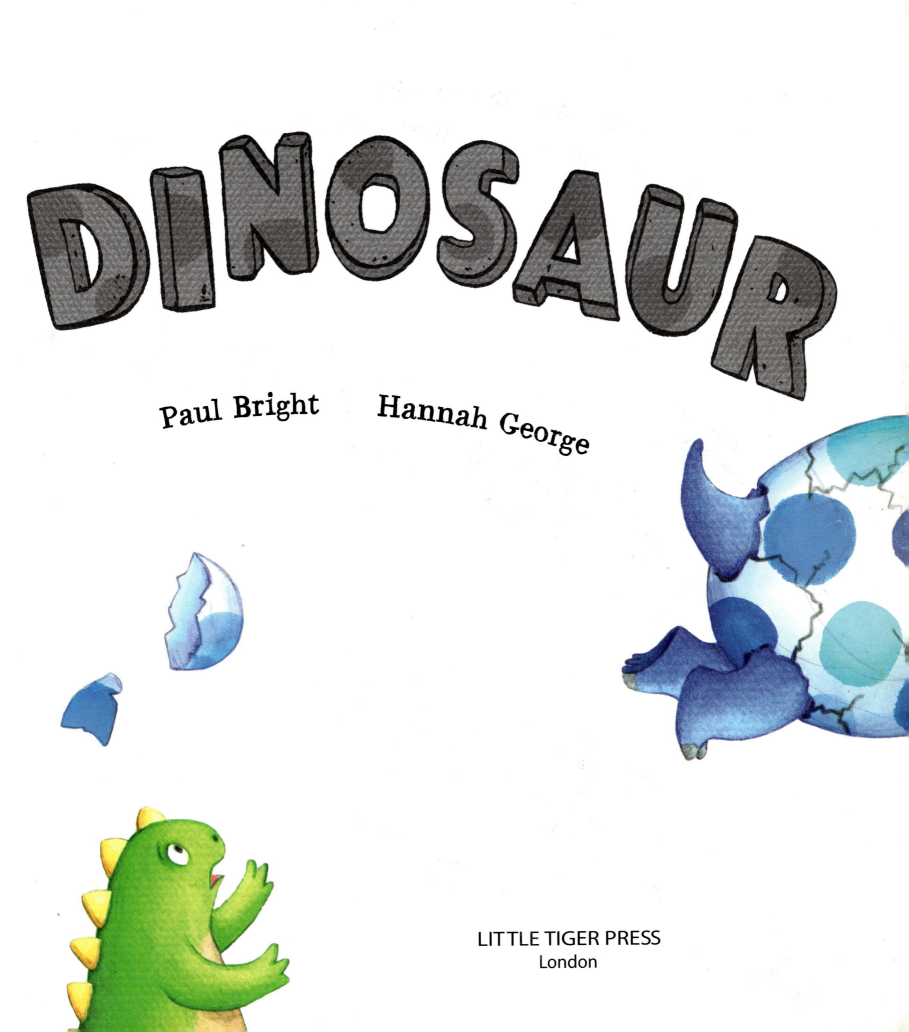

LITTLE TIGER PRESS
London

Down in the valley
where the dinosaurs play,
Meg Mummisaurus laid an egg one day.
Great Grannisaurus said,
"I think it would be best,
To keep it snug and safe
in a dinosaur nest."

So Meg put her egg in a nest by the lake,
But Waggosaurus came, with a SWAGGER
and a SHAKE,
Wobbling the egg . . .

till **Meg** let out a **wail**,

"Watch where you're wagging your **tail**!"

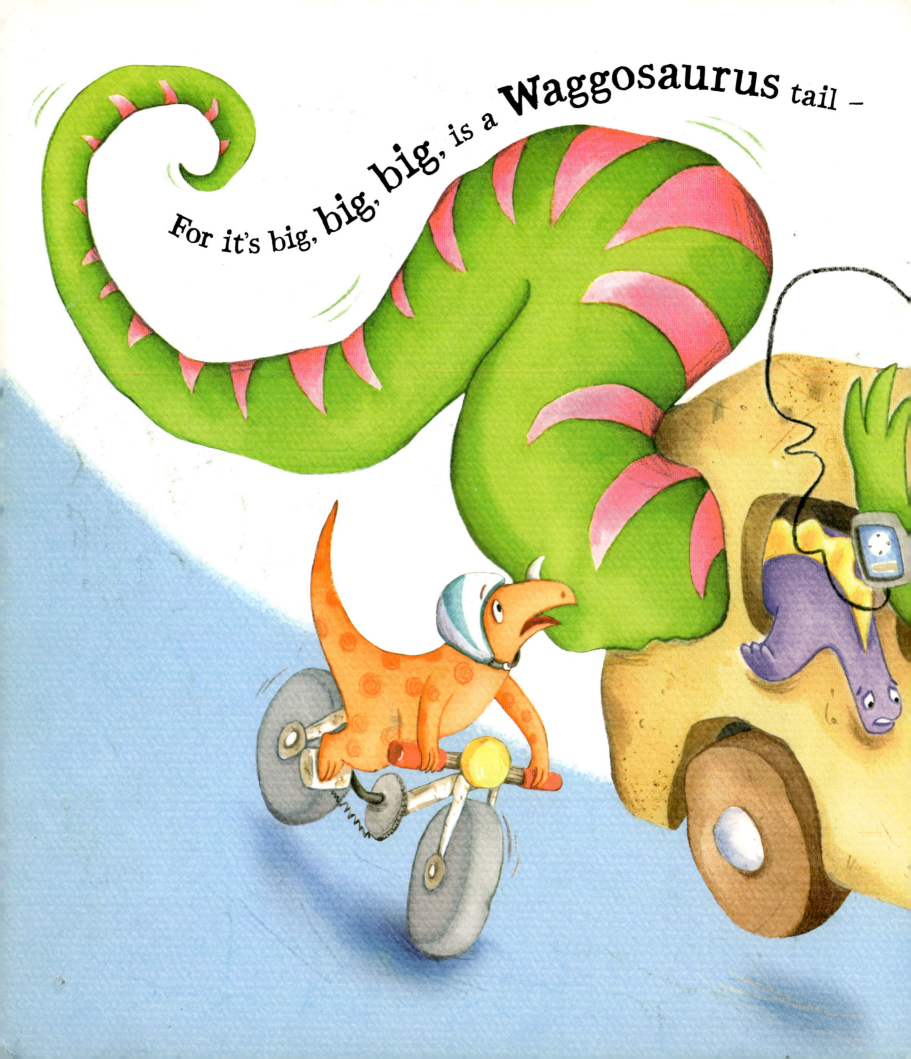

For it's big, **big**, **big**, is a **Waggosaurus** tail –

As big as a **bus**, or a **boulder** or a **whale**!
If you meet a **Waggosaurus** you must tell him, without fail,

"**Watch where you're wagging your tail!**"

So Meg put her egg
in a nest by the swamp,
But Clomposaurus came,
with a STAMP and a STOMP!
The egg began to shake to
the great drumbeat.

"Watch where
you're putting
your feet!"

are Clomposaurus feet –

For they're big, big, big,

A Clomposaurus ballerina you will **never** meet!
If you see a Clomposaurus come stomping down the street,
Shout . . .

"Watch where you're putting your feet!"

So Meg put her egg where
the green grass grows,
But Noseysaurus came,
with his snuffling nose,

SNORTING and SNIFFLING

till Meg had to shout,

"Watch where you're shoving your snout!"

For it's big, big, big, is a Noseysaurus snout,
And should he start to sneeze,
You don't want to hang about.
If you know a Noseysaurus …

Now every **Mummisaurus** needs a snooze or a snack, So **Meg** checked her **egg**, then she said, "I'll soon be back!"

And she went for a walk
by the swamp and the lake,
But that was a **big mistake!**

Eggsciting Tales

For dim Dozysaurus came
lumbering into sight –
A bumble-stumble dinosaur
who's dozy day and night –

Swishing, stomping, snuffling,
with tail and feet and snout.

Come back, Meg!
Protect your egg!
Look out!
Look out!

Look out!

Then the **egg** gave a
crick,

and the **egg** gave a
crack.

A **snout** poked
from the front end
and a **tail** stuck
out the back.

The **egg** stood up,
it gave a
SQUEAK,
and then began
to run!

Crickle,
crackle,
came four feet,
emerging one by one.

"Ouch!" said Noseysaurus, rubbing at his nose.

"Ouch!" said Clomposaurus. "Could you mind my toes!"

"Ouch!"

said Waggosaurus.
"That's my tail,
you know!"

"Run!" said Meg.
"Run, little egg! Go, Spikisaurus.
Go!"

Down in the valley
where the dinosaurs play,
Baby Spikisaurus grows a little more each day.
And all the other dinosaurs say,
"Play just where you like, but...